The Magic Pretzel

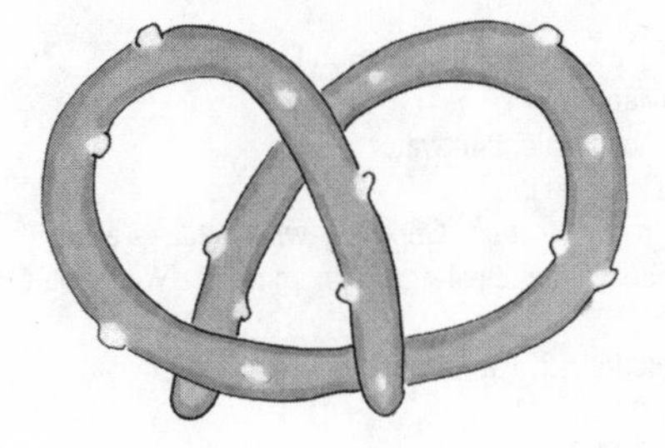

ATHENEUM BOOKS FOR YOUNG READERS
New York London Toronto Sydney Singapore

Atheneum Books for Young Readers
An imprint of Simon & Schuster Children's Publishing Division
1230 Avenue of the Americas
New York, NY 10020

Also available in an Aladdin Paperbacks edition.

Book design by Corinne Allen

The text for this book was set in Weidemann Book.
The illustrations were rendered in Magic Marker, pen,
and imported European wolf spit.

Printed and bound in the United States of America

10 9 8 7 6 5 4 3 2 1

Library of Congress Cataloging-in-Publication Data:
Pinkwater, Daniel Manus, 1941–
The magic pretzel / by Daniel Pinkwater.
p. cm. (Werewolf Club ; #1)
Summary: Fourth-grader Norman Gnormal, who behaves a lot like a dog, finds his first real friends when the principal signs him up for the Werewolf Club at school.
ISBN 0-689-83800-X
[1. Werewolves—Fiction. 2. Humorous stories.] I. Title.
PZ7.P6335 Map 2000
[Fic]—dc21   00-021993

FREQUENTLY ASKED WEREWOLF QUESTIONS

Q: What is a werewolf?

A: A werewolf is a person who turns into a wolf from time to time.

Q: Is that true?

A: Would I lie to you?

Q: What makes a person turn into a werewolf?

A: Everyone knows people turn into werewolves if they are bitten by a werewolf, but you can turn into a werewolf by:

1. thinking about werewolves
2. using a drinking fountain after a werewolf

3. reading a book like this one

4. for no reason at all

Q: What should you do if a werewolf bites you?

A: Go home and wait.

Q: Are werewolves nice?

A: Oh, they are very nice. Of course, their ways are different from ours. Just remember, a bite can be a werewolf's way of saying, "Let's be friends."

Q: Is there any way to stop turning into a werewolf?

A: Yes. One.

Q: What is it?

A: It is the magic pretzel.

Q: The magic pretzel? Does such a thing really exist?

A: No one knows.

MR. GNORMAL VISITS PRINCIPAL PANTALONI

PRINCIPAL PANTALONI

Mr. Gnormal, your son Norman has been growling and threatening to bite other students, and he keeps meat in his desk.

MR. GNORMAL

I can't understand it. Norman has been making such good progress at home. He no longer snaps at us when he has to go to bed, he's quit digging holes in the lawn, and the housebreaking is going great.

PRINCIPAL PANTALONI

I also wanted to ask you, is the drooling something he can't help?

MR. GNORMAL

You mean just before lunchtime?

PRINCIPAL PANTALONI

Yes.

MR. GNORMAL

We find that if we give him a Milk-Bone to chew, it isn't so bad.

PRINCIPAL PANTALONI

I will tell Mrs. Yogami, his teacher.

MR. GNORMAL

Principal Pantaloni, do you have any suggestions for how we should deal with our darling Norman?

PRINCIPAL PANTALONI

I would say, just make sure he has a warm place to sleep, plenty of water whenever he wants . . . and take him for a nice walk a couple of times a day.

MR. GNORMAL

Thank you. It is a fine thing that you take such an interest in our boy.

PRINCIPAL PANTALONI

Education is my life, Mr. Gnormal.

CHAPTER MINUS ONE

THE WEREWOLF CLUB

There was a sheet of paper posted on the bulletin board.

It said:

ARE YOU A WEREWOLF?

DO YOU WANT TO BE ONE?

SIGN-UP SHEET

WATSON ELEMENTARY SCHOOL WEREWOLF CLUB

FIRST MEETING TOMORROW, AFTER SCHOOL, IN MR. TALBOT'S ROOM. SIGN BELOW IF YOU ARE INTERESTED:

There were four signatures:

Ralf Alfa

Billy Furball

Lucy Fang

Norman Gnormal

Wait! I am Norman Gnormal! I never signed up for the Werewolf Club! I did not know any of those other kids. And Mr. Talbot was known as a weird and scary teacher. But there was my name, written in script—as though I had signed it!

I, NORMAN

I'm pretty sure my parents really wanted a dog, but they got me instead. The earliest thing I can remember is playing with a rubber bone on the living room rug. My father would toss the bone, and say, "Fetch, boy! Get the bone, Norman! Good boy!"

I soon found out I could please Mom and Dad by acting like a dog—which I did. And to tell the truth, I liked it. I have to say, I had a happy puppyhood.

They are good parents. They make sure there is plenty of stuff to chew lying around, and they don't make a big deal about baths. At bedtime I get liver treats.

I try to be a good kid and not bark at night.

Things were strange when I first went to school, but I learned to fit in. And it turned out I was not the only one with fleas.

I was in fourth grade when I saw that sign-up sheet. The Werewolf Club! I was curious about it, even though someone else had signed my name.

THAT NIGHT

That night, as I lay in bed, I heard a strange sound from far away.

AWOOOoooo!

AT BREAKFAST

The next day at breakfast: "Dad, are we werewolves?"

"Of course not, Norman. Eat your kibble like a good boy, and you can chew on the tennis ball before school."

MR. TALBOT

This is why Mr. Talbot was thought to be weird and scary by the students at Watson Elementary School. He always wore the following items:

A knitted woolen hat, pulled down low on his head

Blue sunglasses

A thick knitted muffler around his neck and chin

A long raincoat

Woolen gloves or mittens

Five-buckle galoshes

And he wore this outfit winter and summer, indoors and out.

It was said he always brought frozen cheese burritos for lunch, heated them in the school microwave, and ate them without removing his muffler. Thus there were always strands of cheese on his muffler and mittens.

Also, he had a funny way of walking. He sort of loped, almost sideways, with one shoulder lower than the other. He could go pretty fast when he got started.

Most of the kids agreed that this made him a weird and scary teacher, though some thought that Mr. Dracula was scarier.

CHAPTER FOUR

THE WEREWOLF CLUB

I went to the meeting.

There was Mr. Talbot, all covered up, with cheese on him.

There were the three other kids whose names had been on the sign-up sheet.

Ralf Alpha was a natural leader. He was stupid and handsome, with a toothy smile. The moment I saw him, I knew I wanted to be just like him—and couldn't.

Billy Furball was very unsanitary. He seemed sort of . . . soggy. There weren't any flies buzzing around him, but I looked for some.

I had seen Lucy Fang in the schoolyard, wearing sunglasses, tossing corn chips in the air, and catching them in her mouth. She struck me as rather grown-up and sophisticated.

All the kids gave me dirty looks when I came in.

I took a seat in the back.

MR. TALBOT SPEAKS

Mr. Talbot recited a little poem.

"Even a child who is pure of heart,
And does his homework neatly,
May become a wolf when the wolfbane blooms,
And the moon is full, completely."

Then he said, "Welcome, students, to the first meeting of the Watson Elementary School Werewolf Club." Mr. Talbot wrote on the board, WERE-WOLF, LY-CAN-THROPE, TURN-SKIN, WOLF-MAN, VER-SI-PELL-IS, VOLK-LO-DAK, WEE-GEE WEE-GEE OOK-EE OOK-EE." All names of the good old werewolf in different languages," Mr. Talbot said. "I am glad to see you all here. Of course, Norman Gnormal is not actually a werewolf. Our principal, Mr. Pantaloni, signed him up because there isn't a club for boys who think they are dogs."

The other kids turned in their seats and snickered and barked at me.

"Now, students . . . we will not ridicule, bite, torture or abuse Norman, just because he is a mere human. We will have fun in other ways, and learn more about being werewolves. Maybe we will be ready to howl for the whole school at the Midwinter Assembly."

This is the pits, I thought. *I want to be a werewolf too.*

I'M THE WEENIE

"Come on, Billy. Just give me a little nip."

"Euwww. No way. I'm not biting you."

"Come on, have a bite. I'll give you table scraps."

"It's not going to happen, Norman," Billy Furball said. "Werewolves have a strict pecking order, same as regular wolves. Ralf Alfa is the top dog, and I am on the bottom . . . or I was until you showed up."

"So as long as I'm not a real werewolf . . . ?"

"You're the weenie." Billy smiled a big smile. "And don't think Ralf or Lucy will put the tooth on you. They'll just kick your butt—do everything to you except bite you."

"No fair! I want to be a real werewolf!"

"Who wouldn't?"

SO MUCH FUN

I could have quit the Werewolf Club, but it was so much fun!

We had a picnic . . . at midnight . . . in a graveyard! We ran through the streets. We howled under windows and scared people. We knocked over garbage cans.

And when the full moon rolled around . . . the other kids changed. This was the coolest thing of all. They got all furry, and toothy, and strong. They liked to run on all fours.

Of course, I was just the same as always, but a lifetime of being raised as a dog prepared me to keep up with them. I could run pretty fast, and I do a good howl, if I say so myself.

Mr. Talbot, the Werewolf Club sponsor, always

went with us on our official outings . . . and he always wore his long coat, hat, gloves, galoshes, muffler, and blue sunglasses . . . even at night.

WHAT THEY USED TO CALL ME

Even though I was not an actual werewolf, and the other kids in the Werewolf Club treated me as a kind of mascot, it was better than before.

Before, the kids at Watson Elementary School used to give me a certain amount of trouble. These are some the things they used to call me:

Lassie

Rover

Fido

Alpo-breath

Drinks-from-the-toilet

Poochie

Poodle-man

Pound Puppy

Jo-Jo the Dogfaced Boy

Not that I minded, you understand . . . just that the werewolves treated me nicer.

FRIENDS

Slowly, slowly, I was gaining acceptance from the other kids in the Werewolf Club. They were impressed that I could keep up with them on night runs, and go on all fours almost as well as they could.

Ralf Alfa even invited me to his house after school one day. He had some neat werewolf posters and trading cards, and a statue of the Wolf Man from the movie.

Billy Furball offered me half of his liverwurst milkshake.

And Lucy Fang once threatened to bite my nose off and suck out my eyeballs. I could see Ralf and Billy were jealous that she was paying that kind of attention to me.

I was happy. Friends are good. Principal Pantaloni

did the right thing when he signed me up.

Ralf Alfa

Number 1,263
Age: 9 years
Height: 53.5 inches
Weight: 87 pounds
Type of wolf: gray, European forest wolf (extinct)
Number of bites: 4
Outrages: 6
Favorite food: meat
Favorite beverage: Diet Pepsi
Favorite book: *I was a Second Grade Werewolf*
Favorite movie: *The Wolf Man*
Favorite actor/actress: Maria Ouspenskaya
Favorite quotation: "It is not your fault, my son! You were born under an unlucky star!"
Ambition: To bite the President of the United States

AN UN-FULL MOON

Of course, our big doings took place during the full moon—that's when the other kids changed. That's when they got all hairy, and their noses turned into muzzles, and they grew fangs an inch long. But we sometimes went out for a howl during the month, when we looked more or less like ordinary kids . . . except maybe Billy Furball.

We would go out and scare animals at the zoo, or howl under people's windows, or just scamper through the streets, knocking over garbage cans.

We didn't have Mr. Talbot with us when we went on runs like that. He would not have approved of us growling at people in the parking lot of Pizza Universe or Demented Doughnuts.

That's where we were the night we decided to

visit him. Ralf Alfa knew where Mr. Talbot lived. We had never been to his house. We decided to drop in.

"It's a friendly thing to do," Ralf said.

"He likes us. He'll be happy to see us," Lucy said.

"Maybe he has leftovers," Billy Furball said.

"Let's go."

MR. TALBOT'S HOUSE

Mr. Talbot's house was behind a tall iron fence. We couldn't see past the fence because it was all overgrown with bushes and vines. Ralf Alfa pushed the gate open. The front yard was all overgrown too. We could barely tell there was a house.

"Are you sure this is Mr. Talbot's house?" I asked Ralf.

Ralf sniffed the air. "Definitely," he said.

We walked single file along the narrow path. There were weeds and grasses crowding us. The house was old-looking, and dark, and creepy. If we hadn't been the Werewolf Club, we would have been scared for sure.

We saw a dim light coming from one window at the side of the house. And we heard music. Someone was listening to a recording of *Peter and the Wolf,* by Prokofiev.

"Let's peek in," Lucy Fang whispered.

We had to leave the path and struggle through the old dead leaves and dead branches, and some soft mushy places. It was hard to see where we were stepping in the dark, and at times we weren't sure what we stepped on.

Ralf Alfa got to the window first. He stood on tip-toe and peeked in.

"What do you see?" I asked.

Ralf Alfa's eyes were shining in the dim light.

"It's . . . it's . . . it's . . . "

WITHOUT HIS HAT

We crowded together and stood on tiptoe. We could just get our noses above the windowsill. We could see into the room. There was a . . . creature.

It was horrible. It had matted fur and pointy ears. It was shaped sort of like a man, but it wasn't human. It had horrible hairy paws, and long black curved fingernails . . . claws!

Its nose was black, and we could see sharp white teeth.

The creature looked our way. It had scary yellow eyes.

"Oh no! It's a werewolf!"

"Run! Run!"

We screamed. We ran. Terror gripped us.

"Ahhhhh!" Ralf Alfa screamed.

"Eeeeek!" Lucy Fang screamed.

"Mommeee!" Billy Furball screamed.

"Woof! Woof! Woof!" I barked. Often I surprise myself by reverting to my early childhood training.

We ran all the way to the gate. Then Ralf Alfa said, "Wait a second! We're werewolves ourselves . . . except for Norman. Why are we running?"

"I was wondering the same thing," said Mr. Talbot, who was standing on the porch. "Now that you know my secret, you may as well come in and have some hot ginger ale."

HIS SECRET?

Mr. Talbot's house was very nice, and modern, with lots of wood-grain paneling and metal-and-vinyl furniture. There were pictures on the walls, mostly of forests by moonlight, and one photograph of an old lady with one earring, and a scarf on her head. It was autographed. "From Mommy . . . it is not your fault," it said.

Mr. Talbot served us hot ginger ale, which was fairly awful. He seemed uncomfortable and nervous.

"Well, now you know my secret," Mr. Talbot said.

"What secret?" Ralf Alfa said. "You're a werewolf. We assumed as much. Why the big deal?"

"You're werewolves," Mr. Talbot said. "You turn into wolves, you turn into kids. It's a normal healthy thing. But look at me. There's no full moon. You guys aren't in wolf mode. But here I am all hairy. I'm stuck in between. Not a wolf—not a man. It makes me want to howl."

"I can see where that would be different," Lucy Fang said.

"May I have some more hot ginger ale?" Billy Furball asked.

THE CURSE OF VON SWEENY

"It's no joke getting on a bus, or coming to work every morning, when you look like this," Mr. Talbot said. "People tend not to understand."

"I think you look very nice," Lucy Fang said.

"Thank you," Mr. Talbot said. "But most people don't know how to act. If I hear one more Little Red Riding Hood joke, I will bite someone."

"I think if you just went around looking . . . like you do . . . people would get used to it," I said.

"No, it's better for me to keep covered up," Mr. Talbot said. "Society isn't ready for a full-time wolf man."

"Would you tell us how this happened to you?" Ralf Alfa said.

"I was cursed," Mr. Talbot said.

"Cursed?"

"Cursed. By Lance Von Sweeny, my own half brother."

"He cursed you?"

"Yes."

"And now you can't change?"

"Can't."

"And your half brother?"

"Thinks it's funny."

"Wow."

THE MAGIC PRETZEL

"Isn't there some way to get uncursed?" Billy Furball asked. We all looked at him because he had asked an intelligent question.

"There is one way only," Mr. Talbot said. "A secret ritual—but I'd need a magic pretzel for it to work."

"A magic pretzel?"

"If I had one, I could reverse the curse."

"Reverse the curse . . . reverse the curse," Billy Furball chanted. He had gone back to being his normal idiot self.

"Where can you get a magic pretzel?" Ralf Alfa asked.

"My half brother, Lance Von Sweeny, has one—possibly the only one on earth."

"And he won't give it to you?"

"Ha!"

"Where does he keep this magic pretzel?" Lucy Fang asked.

"He keeps it in a special burglar-proof case in the Museum of the Pretzel, which he owns. The magic one, said to have belonged to Alexander the Great, is the only good thing in the whole place."

"Burglar-proof, maybe—but not werewolf-proof," Ralf Alfa said.

"That's just what I was thinking," I said.

THE ACCURSED VON SWEENY

"My half brother, Von Sweeny, is a dangerous man," Mr. Talbot said.

"Dangerous in what way? And how did he curse you?" we asked.

"Oh, he has a magic chicken. Its name is Suzanne. He can wave the chicken at you, and poof! You're cursed. Then he mocks you. Only last night, he was mocking me when we had dinner at Mommy's house."

"You see him at dinner at your . . . mommy's . . . house?"

"Of course."

"Your mother?"

"Who else would I call Mommy?"

"Does she know your half brother put a curse on you?"

"I suppose she knows. He mocks me about it all the time."

"Can't your . . . uh, mommy tell Lance Von Sweeny, your half brother, to take the curse off you?"

"I suppose. But she would never do anything that might make Lance angry."

"Because she's afraid of being cursed with Suzanne the chicken?"

"No, because Lance is her favorite. She always liked him best because he smells better than I do, and doesn't get cheese all over himself."

AT THE MUSEUM

The very next Saturday, the members of the Watson Elementary Werewolf Club walked eight blocks, took two buses, and arrived at the Museum of the Pretzel. It was on Nemo Boulevard, where most of the stores were empty, and there were weeds growing up through cracks in the sidewalk.

Mr. Talbot came along, but thought it best not to go in. "I will wait for you here at the bus stop," he said. "My half brother might get mad, and mock me or something."

The museum was in a former store, with two big display windows. There were a lot of hand-painted signs taped to the windows: MUSEUM OF THE PRETZEL. TREASURES FROM THE ANCIENT WORLD. FORTUNE-

TELLING CHICKEN. USED COMIC BOOKS FOR SALE. TROPICAL FISH. DINOSAUR TEETH.

The signs were red and yellow, and there were colored Christmas lights. It seemed like a cool place, actually, and not scary.

The idea was, we were going to talk to Lance Von Sweeny, half brother of Mr. Talbot, and see if we could get him to take off the partial-werewolf curse.

We went into the Museum of the Pretzel. Standing just inside the doorway, with his hands on his hips and his legs apart, was someone who looked a lot like Mr. Talbot . . . only he was about eight feet tall!

OH, NO!

Not that many people have to face a giant, let alone one who is evil and has cursed your club's faculty sponsor. I should mention that he was not just tall—he was strong-looking, and his shoes seemed to be the size of sports cars.

"May I help you?" the giant said. You could feel his voice in your teeth.

We just stood there, feeling tiny. None of us could say a word.

"Feel free to look around," the giant said. "Things in the front of the store are for sale, and the back part is the Museum of the Pretzel. Look, but don't touch."

The front of the store was full of neat things: rubber rats, screaming-head gummy candy, glow-in-

the-dark earmuffs, plastic chicken feet that fit over your shoes . . . all sorts of stuff.

I was surprised to hear my own voice. I was wondering which of us would get up the courage to speak to the giant—and it turned out to be me! "Are you Lance Von Sweeny, half brother of our friend Mr. Talbot?"

"Oh, no! Friends of my silly half brother! So you didn't come in to buy anything? I might have known. Where is he? Hiding at the bus stop as usual?"

BROTHER AND A HALF

Lance Von Sweeny, Mr. Talbot's half brother, was more like a brother and a half. He was big enough to scare anyone, yet he seemed quite friendly.

"Go out and drag my half brother in here," Von Sweeny said. "Tell him I know he's out there, so he may as well come in."

Ralf Alfa went to get Mr. Talbot.

Lance Von Sweeny was showing us Suzanne, the fortune-telling chicken, when Ralf Alfa came back, dragging Mr. Talbot by the hand.

The way the chicken worked was this: You'd put a quarter in a slot on the outside of her cage. This would cause a little bell to ring. The chicken would then take a tightly rolled piece of paper out of a box and drop it in a hole—it would slide out into your hand. Then a few kernels of corn would drop into a cup, and she'd eat them. We all put in quarters, and got little rolled-up fortunes.

"Don't trust him!" Mr. Talbot said. "He'd as soon put a curse on you as look at you!"

IT'S EDUCATIONAL

Lance Von Sweeny threw a switch, and spotlights came on in the back part of the store. "The Museum of the Pretzel," he said. "Please approach, and have a look around. It's highly educational.

"Here we have an ancient Egyptian pretzel. This is a fragment of the Great Pretzel of China. Here is the smallest pretzel ever made. (Look through the magnifying glass.) And holding up the ceiling is the largest pretzel in existence. Here are pretzels which bear an uncanny resemblance to famous people, Winston Churchill, Attila the Hun, Richard Nixon, Elvis, and the dog in the taco commercials. In this case you can see the pretzel of the future, containing a tiny computer chip. On the walls, please observe the series of paintings, 'Pretzels: Mankind's Friends Through the Ages.'"

Lance Von Sweeny unlocked a case and removed a pretzel that glowed with a greenish light. "This is the magic pretzel, once the property of Alexander the Great, and the most valuable object here. Take it with you."

"Take it? I can take it?" Mr. Talbot asked.

"With my blessing," Lance Von Sweeny said. "Remember to bring it back when you're done with it." Mr. Talbot was almost crying. "I've misjudged you."

"You got that right, bro," Lance Von Sweeny said.

HORNSWOGGLED

We were on the bus, heading toward home. Mr. Talbot had a little white bakery box, tied with string. In it was the magic pretzel.

"Mr. Talbot, I have to say, your half brother seems to be a nice guy, and not evil at all," Lucy Fang said.

"He's very big too," Billy Furball said.

"He let you have the magic pretzel, and he gave us these neat whistles shaped like pickles," Ralf Alfa said.

"And we got fortunes from Suzanne the chicken," I said.

We had almost forgotten the little, tightly rolled pieces of paper with our fortunes on them. We dug them out of our pockets, unrolled them, and read them.

Lucy's read: "'Give us the pretzel,' they came to say."

Then Billy's: "Of course, of course, just take it away."

And Ralf's: "You wouldn't trick us or do something foxy?"

Mine read: "Oh yes, I would, just look in the boxy."

Mr. Talbot snapped the string on the bakery box and flipped open the lid. Inside was a stale cupcake, left over from Halloween. It had orange icing, a full moon, and a black bat on it. There was a card in the box which read:

SUCKERS!

"We've been hornswoggled!" Mr. Talbot shouted.

DONE A BUNK

When we got back to the Museum of the Pretzel, all the Christmas lights were off, the door was locked, and the signs were gone. Sheets of newspaper had been taped to the insides of the windows, and painted on the windows in white paint were the words: OUT OF BUSINESS. GONE TO PERU. GOOD-BYE TO ALL OUR CUSTOMERS.

"He's bolted, absconded, sneaked away, high-tailed it, shoved off, fled, departed, defected, skedaddled, and split!" Mr. Talbot said.

"You mean he ran away?" we asked.

"He's done a bunk!" Mr. Talbot cried. "He's taken French leave, vanished, bugged out, skipped, boogied, vacated. He's left the building. He's out of here. He's a dot. He's history."

"You mean he's not at this location anymore?"

"Yes," Mr. Talbot said. "And he has the magic pretzel. He left me here with nothing but a stale Halloween cupcake."

"May I have it?" Billy Furball asked.

BACK ON THE BUS

"How can you think of eating at a time like this?" Mr. Talbot asked.

"I don't want to eat it. I want to sniff it," Billy Furball said.

"Sniff it?" Mr. Talbot asked.

"Lance Von Sweeny must have handled it," Billy Furball said. "Once I get a whiff of his scent, I will be able to tell you which way he went."

Billy Furball brought the stale Halloween cupcake up under his nose, and inhaled. "I am getting definite traces of dried-up SpaghettiOs, cookie crumbs, barbecue sauce, and dirt!"

"You're smelling your own shirt!" Lucy Fang said. "Some werewolf you are."

I snatched the cupcake from Billy Furball. "Give

that here!" I said. "Not for nothing did my father send me to obedience school. I am an expert tracker and scent hound." I sniffed the cupcake. I could smell Lance Von Sweeny clear as day. Then I shoved my trained nose out the window of the moving bus, and sniffed deeply.

"He went thataway!" I said. "Pull the stop-the-bus cord, and let's get after him!" I felt a warm surge of gratitude to my father for having given me a good education.

AFTER THE PARSNIP!

The Werewolf Club piled out of the bus. For a minute or two I had to run in circles, sniffing the ground and then sniffing the air. This is how we were taught to do it at the Barbara Woofhouse Obedience Academy. Then, when I was sure I had the scent, I pointed stiffly up the street.

"Let's go!" I said.

"Yes! Let's go!" Mr. Talbot said. "Let's catch him! Catch the hornswoggler!"

We took off at a run, charging along the sidewalk.

"Look for a giant parsnip!" Mr. Talbot said. He was huffing and puffing, and gasped the words out between huffs.

"A giant parsnip?"

"My evil half brother will be driving his car. It

looks like a giant parsnip. He bought it secondhand. It was formerly a delivery car for Veggie Express."

"The vegetarian-dinner delivery place?"

"Yes."

"'You Ring—We Bring?'"

"That's the one."

"And he has one of those neat vegetable cars they use?"

"He has."

"Wow. Lance Von Sweeny may be evil, but he does so many cool things!"

RUNNING, RUNNING, RUNNING

All this time we were running, running, running. I was out in front, following the scent. There were a million smells in the city, but I was able to ignore everything but the slightly chickeny scent of Lance Von Sweeny. I ran, and sniffed, the others following.

But if Von Sweeny was in a car, we would never catch him if he kept moving. Those veggie cars can make thirty-five miles an hour with a fresh battery. All we could do was keep after him and hope he'd stop somewhere.

RUNNING, RUNNING, RUNNING, RUNNING

Everybody was a good runner. Even Mr. Talbot, who was on the fat side, was able to keep up.

We had been running for more than an hour. Every so often we'd all sort of collapse, and rest for a minute or two. Then I'd feel my nose rise into the air, and the rest of my body would follow it—getting me up off the sidewalk, and moving, following the scent—and the others would come after me.

We ran through city streets. We ran into the suburbs, where there were more trees and fewer houses. We ran out into the country where there were lots more trees and lots fewer houses.

It was getting dark. I sniffed. We ran.

No one complained. No one wanted to quit. No one doubted that I had the true scent and we were following Von Sweeny. They trusted me.

A GRAVEYARD

We ran through a graveyard. It was a big one, with a road going through it. The scent led me there, and I followed it. The other kids and Mr. Talbot followed me. It was getting quite dark.

"Ohhh! Look!"

The moon! The moon was rising! It was a full moon! We had forgotten all about it.

"Awooo!" someone said. Then someone else said, "Awooo!"

They were changing. The other kids. They were changing.

Still running, they changed. Their noses got long. Their teeth became fangs. They pitched forward as they ran, and their arms and legs became long and thin and strong and hairy.

"Awooo!"

The moon was big, and rising fast. Cold white light on the gravestones.

"Awooo!"

We stretched as we ran. We sucked in big gulps of air. It felt good. We flew. We were not tired. We could not get tired. We were strong, and light, and hard and fast. We could see in the dark.

We?

WE?

I was stretching way out with my arms, and pulling myself forward. At the same time, my legs were coming up under me, pulled up like a coiled spring. Then I'd push with my legs and shoot forward while reaching out with my arms. It felt like flying.

The moon shone on my silver fur, and I drew in deep, deep breaths of cold air through my long snout. I could feel my brother wolves and sister wolf running with me. No longer was I the only one who could catch the scent of Von Sweeny. We could all smell him. We could almost smell what he was thinking. We could smell what color shirt he had on. A mostly pink Hawaiian one.

Wait! Wait just a second! Wait just a howling, barking, drooling second!

What had happened here?

I had changed! I had changed with the others. I was a wolf! A werewolf! It had happened! I was one!

It felt great.

FOUND A PARSNIP

Mr. Talbot was about two miles behind us when we found it. He had the heart but not the legs.

There was the parsnip car, parked on a quiet street, outside a nice-looking little house. We hid ourselves in some bushes, and whispered.

"Shall we wait for Mr. Talbot?" "No. Let's rush in!" "Rush into somebody's house?"

"We have to. Lance Von Sweeney might escape by the back door or something."

"But it's wrong to just burst into somebody's house."

"It's wrong to refuse to lend your half brother a magic pretzel when he needs it."

"We could be taken for burglars."

"We're werewolves. We'll scare the snot out of him."

"Okay, let's do it. Remember to growl when we get in."

We rushed the house and crowded through the front door, growling and waving our paws in the air.

In the house we found Lance Von Sweeny and a little woman, with big earrings and a scarf tied around her head.

The old lady spoke with an accent, "Ahhh! Werewolves!

The little children of the night. Come, darlings! Have some borscht."

BORSCHT?

"Lance, darling. Get bowls and spoons for your little friends," the old woman said. "So cute, little wolf-things—I could just pinch your whiskers, little sweetie pies."

Lance Von Sweeny got bowls and spoons and napkins, and set places for us, while the old woman stirred a big pot of something weird and purple.

"Who is this woman?" Ralf Alfa whispered.

"Lance Von Sweeny does what she tells him," I whispered back.

"So she would have to be . . . "

"Mommy," a voice behind us said. It was Mr. Talbot.

"Lawrence!" the old woman said. "Look! We have werewolves to supper! Come, darling—eat borscht."

Borscht turns out to be soup. This borscht was made from shredded beets, if you can believe that, with a lump of sour cream in the middle.

These are the ratings the Werewolf Club gave to Mr. Talbot's mommy's borscht:

Ralf Alfa: Ick!

Lucy Fang: Ack!

Norman Gnormal: Ook!

Billy Furball: Yum!

Mr. Talbot: This is why I left home.

CHAPTER THIRTY-ONE

TABLE TALK

"So? What have you been doing, my fine boys?" Mr. Talbot's and Lance Von Sweeny's mother asked.

Mr. Talbot lifted his hands in the air and moaned, "I am trapped halfway between wolf and man!"

"It is not your fault, my son," his mommy told him.

"You were born under an unlucky star. And how has your week been, Lance?"

"Lawrence has been bothering me again, Mommy," Lance Von Sweeny said.

"Don't bother your half brother, Lawrence," Mommy said.

"May I have some more borscht?" Billy Furball asked.

Even Lance Von Sweeny looked at Billy Furball with amazement.

"What a fine young semihuman canine you are," Mommy said, and patted Billy Furball on the head.

"All Mr. Talbot wants is to borrow the magic pretzel so he can take off the curse Mr. Von Sweeny put on him," Billy Furball said.

"Is this true?" Mommy asked. "You won't lend your half brother a pretzel?"

"It's a special pretzel, Mommy," Lance Von Sweeny said.

"Lance, you have to learn to share your things. Let your half brother have the pretzel."

"Yes, Mommy."

THAT'S IT?

Lance Von Sweeny dug the magic pretzel out of his pocket and handed it to Mr. Talbot. "You had better not mess this up, the way you did my comic books," he said.

"Whoopee! I'm almost uncursed!" Mr. Talbot shouted. "Let's go out in the backyard and do the ritual!"

"Wait, darlings!" Mommy said. "Don't you want to have some jellied calves' feet first?"

The four werewolves, Mr. Talbot, and Lance Von Sweeny struggled, pushed, and punched each other trying to get through the narrow doorway into the backyard.

THE RITUAL

Mr. Talbot made us all stand in a circle around him. He held the magic pretzel over his head and recited these words:

"Under the full moon, at the witching hour,
The magic pretzel lends its power.
Undo the curse's evil work.
And if anyone stops us, may he drown in borscht."

Then he made us hold our arms out and spin counterclockwise until we were too dizzy to stand. We lay on the ground until Mommy came out with herring and crackers for everyone.

"It is done!" Mr. Talbot said. "The curse is lifted!

No more will I be trapped halfway between man and wolf!"

"He looks just the same," Lucy Fang whispered.

"Nothing happened," Ralf Alfa said.

"Don't say anything," I said. "He's happy, and that's all that matters."

"May I have another piece of herring?" Billy Furball asked.

"I have to walk my chicken," Lance Von Sweeny said.

"I'll see you next week, Mommy."

"It is not your fault, my son!" Mommy said.

THE NEXT DAY

The next day at school, the members of the Werewolf Club were sitting together in the lunchroom.

"Did you see Mr. Talbot today?" Ralf Alfa asked.

"Yes. He looks the same as he did last night under the full moon," I said.

"He looks the same as he always did," Lucy Fang said.

"Except he isn't wearing the hat, and raincoat, and sunglasses, and scarf, and gloves, and galoshes," I said.

"He's happy. He doesn't feel trapped between being a man and being a wolf anymore," Ralf Alfa said.

"Adults are strange," Lucy Fang said.

"It seems the magic pretzel didn't really have any magic powers," I said.

"And it tasted quite stale," Billy Furball said.

END